GRANDMA
COMES TO STAY

Ifeoma Onyefulu

F
FRANCES LINCOLN
CHILDREN'S BOOKS

This is Stephanie.

Stephanie is three.

To Stephanie and her grandmother,
without whose help I wouldn't have written this book

First published in Great Britain in 2009 and the USA in 2010 by
Frances Lincoln Children's Books,
4 Torriano Mews,
Torriano Avenue,
London NW5 2RZ
www.franceslincoln.com

British Library Cataloguing in Publication
Data available on request

ISBN: 978-1-84507-865-2

Set in Green

Printed in China
1 3 5 7 9 8 6 4 2

Stephanie lives here with her mum,
dad and big sister, Mary.

Stephanie's friends have come to play
but all Stephanie wants to do is

sweep the floor...

arrange the chairs...

tidy up...

help with the shopping
at Kaneshie market...

and help Mummy with the cooking.

Then Stephanie sits down
and does a lovely drawing...
because someone special
is coming to stay.

Grandma!

Grandma says "Thank you" to Stephanie for working so hard, and gives her a box of pencils.

Then Grandma, Stephanie, Mary, Mum
and Dad sit down at the table for a meal.

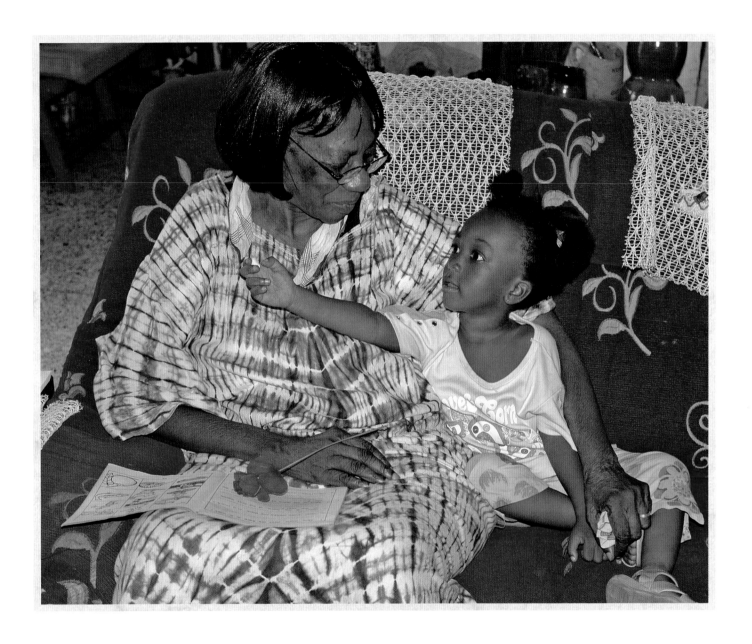

Later, Grandma reads Stephanie her favourite book.

Next morning, Grandma shows
Stephanie how to tie a wrapper...

and a head-dress.

Then Stephanie shows Grandma
how to kick a ball...

ride a bike...

use a counting book...

play with dolls...

do the ironing...

and play the drum.

In the afternoon, Grandma takes Stephanie
and Mary to see real-life drummers and dancers
at Osu Homowo festival.

And at bedtime, Grandma tells Stephanie
a wonderful story about a magic drum.

Next morning, it's time for Grandma
to say goodbye. "Come back soon,
Grandma!" say Stephanie and Mary.